BIONICLE®

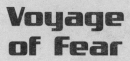

Voyage of Fear

BIONICLE®

FIND THE POWER,
LIVE THE LEGEND

The legend comes alive in these exciting BIONICLE® books:

BIONICLE™ Chronicles
#1 Tale of the Toa
#2 Beware the Bohrok
#3 Makuta's Revenge
#4 Tales of the Masks

The Official Guide to BIONICLE™

BIONICLE™ Collector's Sticker Book

BIONICLE™: Mask of Light

BIONICLE® Adventures
#1 Mystery of Metru Nui
#2 Trial by Fire
#3 The Darkness Below
#4 Legends of Metru Nui

BIONICLE®

Voyage of Fear

by Greg Farshtey

SCHOLASTIC INC.
New York   Toronto   London   Auckland   Sydney
Mexico City   New Delhi   Hong Kong   Buenos Aires

For Jackina, who makes
the voyage worthwhile

ISBN 0-439-68022-0

12 11 10 9 8 7 6 5 4 3   5 6 7 9/0

Printed in the U.S.A.
First printing, October 2004

The City Of Metru Nui

INTRODUCTION

Tahu, Toa Nuva of Fire, was troubled. He stood, as he had for many hours, on the steep slope of the Mangai volcano. His eyes scanned the terrain below him, observing dozens of Matoran hard at work. But nowhere in the crowd did he spot the being he wished to see.

The sun had risen and set twice since Turaga Vakama had completed his last tale. It had been an amazing story of how six Toa Metru had risked great danger to save the Matoran from a terrible plot. Despite shocking betrayal and the tragic death of a great hero, they had succeeded in helping the residents of Metru Nui escape from the doomed city.

Although his tale had revealed many secrets, it had left many more mysteries unsolved. When the Toa Metru left the city, they carried only six Matoran with them. These six, like the rest of the city's population, had been rendered unconscious by the evil Makuta and placed inside silver spheres. Yet there were more than six Matoran on Mata Nui — how had they made their way to the island? And what had happened to all the rest who had lived in Metru Nui?

The answers remained elusive, because Turaga Vakama had vanished. No Toa or Matoran had seen the village elder in days. After much debate, Tahu, Gali, and Pohatu had agreed to stay on guard against any threat, while Takanuva, Kopaka, Onua and Lewa quietly searched the island.

Tahu turned to see the Toa Nuva of Water approaching. "Any word?" asked Gali.

"None, and I do not like this," said Tahu. "Turaga Vakama is the leader of my village. I should be out looking for him."

"I understand. But of all Toa, the Matoran look to you for strength and inspiration. Seeing you nearby makes them feel secure. You know the others will do their very best. They will call if they need our aid."

Kopaka's voice came from above and behind them. "I believe I have found our answer."

Both Toa turned to see their friend traveling to greet them via ice bridge. Along with him came Turaga Nokama of Ga-Koro, Turaga Nuju of Ko-Koro, and Matoro, the villager who translated Nuju's peculiar language of grunts, whistles, and gestures.

"There is no need for a search," Nokama said. "Vakama left to spend time alone with his thoughts. He is safe and will return when his spirit is at peace once more."

"Why would he leave without telling anyone?" demanded Tahu.

"With your heart so full of questions, Tahu, would you have let him go?" Nokama asked. "He told myself and the others who fought beside him on Metru Nui. Now we are telling you, and asking that you respect how hard it is has been for Vakama to relive the past through his tales. Give him his time."

Nuju whistled and ran through a rapid series of hand gestures. Matoro nodded and said, "The Turaga says you have learned all you need to about Metru Nui. You should leave Vakama alone now."

Gali shook her head. She looked directly at Nokama as she said, "No. We will not travel to the city of legends with mysteries hanging like a cloud over our heads. I respect the grief Turaga Vakama must feel, but it is more than time that we knew all."

Nokama had always been known for her wisdom. She knew it was pointless to argue with Gali, but she had seen how tired and weak telling his tales had left Vakama. There was only one answer.

"Very well, Toa of Water," she said finally. "Gather your brothers and I will tell you the next chapter of our story."

That night, they assembled around a fire on the beach near Ga-Koro — seven Toa, five Turaga, Matoro, and Hahli, who now served as Chronicler for the Matoran. They waited in silence for Nokama to speak.

"You must remember what had gone before," the Turaga of Water began, her voice little more than a whisper. "Metru Nui had fallen, shattered by storm and earthquake. All of the Matoran had been cast into a deathlike sleep from which we could not awaken them. But we had managed to take six of them, still in their spheres, with the intent to go back for the rest in the future.

"Matau had been able to strap the spheres to the underside of a Vahki transport vehicle, making it seaworthy. Now we sailed through a crack in the Great Barrier, leaving Metru Nui behind in a desperate search for a place of safety for all the Matoran. But where we were going, and what dangers we would face along the way, no one could say. . . ."

"I hate this," muttered Onewa. "I really do."

The Toa Metru of Stone looked around. The other Toa were spread out on their makeshift boat, keeping an eye out for trouble. Matau was in the cockpit struggling to keep the modified Vahki transport on course. All of them were too busy to take notice of his complaint.

"I said —" he began, more loudly.

"We heard," replied Nuju, Toa of Ice. "Other than the fact that we are sailing through a narrow tunnel in a vehicle not designed for travel by water, which could sink at any moment . . . what is bothering you?"

Onewa gestured at the other Toa. "This. All of this! Our city is in danger, the Matoran are imprisoned . . . and we are running away!"

Nuju shook his head. "Our city is shattered, Onewa, possibly beyond repair. We are doing the only thing we can do — trying to find a place for the Matoran to begin again."

"And that's another thing," grumbled Onewa. "Vakama says, 'Sail through the Great Barrier,' and off we go. We don't even know where we're going!"

"We are sailing to someplace far from Metru Nui, filled with new challenges and a new chance at life," answered Nuju. "The way will be long and filled with danger. We may not all survive to walk the surface of that land."

"How do you know?"

"The same way I know that you will not stop complaining until our voyage is over," said Nuju. "I know everything."

Matau turned the wheel sharply to keep the transport from slamming into a rock wall. Even with the spheres keeping it buoyant and the insect-like legs of the vehicle acting as oars, this thing floated about as well as the average Po-Matoran. He had driven just about every kind of transport there was in Metru Nui, at one time or another, but never anything that felt like such a disaster waiting to happen.

Still, what choice did they have? They had defeated Makuta, just barely, but not before he had succeeded in draining the city's power plant of all energy. Tremors were rocking Metru Nui, bringing down buildings and chutes. Vahki order enforcement squads were all over, still trying to fulfill their last orders: Stop the Toa at all costs! Given all that, there really hadn't been time to stop off in Ga-Metru for a proper boat.

Be a Toa-hero, I said, Matau thought. *See exciting new places! Quick-save others! Almost get crushed by a giant plant and hard-stomped by Dark Hunters! What was I thinking?*

Whenua, Toa of Earth, had not spoken a word since the boat sailed through the Great Barrier and into the tunnel. Ordinarily, he would have been consumed by questions. Who had made this tunnel? Where did it lead? Were the light-stones that provided illumination a natural part of the rock walls, or had someone embedded them there?

Archivists were always asking why. That was part of their job. Becoming a Toa Metru had not dulled that part of Whenua. In fact, it was memories of his past life that weighed on him. The Archives were behind him now, having suffered who knew how much damage in the earthquake. Exhibits might have been wrecked, or worse, their contents set free.

Having spent most of his life as an Onu-Matoran, he knew his duty was to preserve and protect the living museum of Metru Nui. But as a Toa Metru, he had a greater obligation now. He had to serve and defend all the metru, not just his home. His friends were depending on him, and the sleeping Matoran were as well.

But when he turned his eyes back toward the tunnel entrance, he could not help but wish that he had been in the Archives when the disaster struck. *That is where I belong*, he said to himself.

*   *   *

Vakama, too, had been quiet since the journey began. He stood at the bow of the vessel, watching for dangers ahead. Nokama stood beside him, looking with wonder at their surroundings.

"Have you ever pondered who built all of this, Vakama?" she asked. "The Great Barrier, this tunnel . . . were there Matoran in the dim past who constructed these things, or did the Great Beings themselves create them?"

When Vakama didn't reply, she turned to look at him. There was a look in his eyes she had come to know all too well in their adventures together. No enemy could strike harder at Vakama than he struck at himself.

"We did all we could," the Toa of Water said gently. "We saved those we could save, Vakama, and one day we will save all the rest. Toa Lhikan would have been — *was* proud of you."

Vakama started at the mention of the Toa's name. Lhikan had been a hero of Metru Nui when these six had been simple Matoran. Betrayed and ambushed, he had sacrificed his Toa power to bring six Toa Metru into being. As a Turaga, he had aided them in their fight against Makuta. But it was his final memory of Lhikan which pained him the most — the noble figure taking a bolt of darkness meant for Vakama and perishing.

"You're right, of course, Nokama. But I keep thinking Lhikan would have found a way to save the city from this cataclysm."

"He did," Nokama replied. "He found us. Remember what he said? 'Save the heart of the city.' He knew the buildings and chutes and statues were not what mattered. It's the Matoran who gave life to Metru Nui, and the Matoran we must fight to save."

Nokama placed a hand on his arm and smiled. "Any Ga-Matoran can tell you that you cannot sail a boat if you are looking behind all the time. You have to look ahead."

"Then let's do that," said Vakama, "starting with this battered Vahki transport. It needs a name."

He picked up his mask-making tool and

swiftly seared a series of Matoran letters on the side of the craft. When he was done, Nokama leaned over his shoulder to see what he had written. It was one simple word:

Lhikan.

The voyage of the *Lhikan* had followed a pretty straight and level course so far. The tunnel widened as the Toa traveled further along. With no turnoffs, there was no way to go astray. But all that was about to change.

Matau slowed the boat to a crawl. Up ahead, the tunnel forked. Both passages looked the same to him: dark, creepy, and about as inviting as the thought of being stranded in a broken chute with Nuju.

"Which way?" the Toa of Air asked no one in particular.

Nokama looked at Vakama. He was straining, but his visions of the future did not come on command. They appeared at random and he wasn't seeing anything now. "I don't know," he answered. "I'm not getting a feeling about either direction."

"Too bad there are no carving-signs saying, 'This Way to Safe Spot,'" said Matau. "I say we go left."

"Why?"

"Because we hardly ever go left," Matau answered, already turning the craft.

"That . . . that is the most ridiculous reason to choose a future path I have ever heard," snapped Nuju. "The course of our mission is being decided by the Toa of Air's desire for variety?"

"I say left," Matau repeated, smiling.

The transport edged into the left passage. It was not even halfway through the tunnel mouth when the liquid protodermis all around began to bubble. The temperature shot up in a split second. Onewa glanced over the side and saw that the transport was starting to melt. He didn't even want to think about what might be happening to the Matoran spheres.

"Back up!" he shouted. "Get us out of here!"

Up ahead, something breached the waves with a powerful roar. The Toa Metru got a glimpse of bright green eyes, a massive body, a mouth large enough to swallow the transport whole, and skin that radiated intense heat. Then the creature crashed back beneath the boiling liquid.

"Right. I definitely say right," Matau muttered, throwing the craft into reverse. Once it was out of the passage, he turned so hard he almost split the craft in two and shot into the other tunnel.

"What was that?" asked Nuju, more stunned than he wanted to admit.

"An illusion?" suggested Nokama. "Something to make us turn back?"

Onewa shook his head. "The damage to the transport is real. My guess is the rest was real as well."

"We'll take turns as lookout, then," said Vakama. "If there are things like that in here, we will need to be on our guard."

Nokama signaled to Matau to stop the

craft. "I am going to check on the condition of the spheres. If they start to leak . . ."

She didn't need to finish her thought. If the spheres leaked, the Matoran inside could drown. She leaped over the side and into the liquid protodermis. It was warmer than she expected, far more than the ocean around Metru Nui had been. It was also surprisingly clear, almost like the purified protodermis that flowed through Ga-Metru.

She swam around the bottom of the transport, checking over each of the spheres. Apparently, they were well made, because it did not look like immersion in the boiling protodermis had done much harm. One of the transport's legs had almost melted clean through and would need repairs.

Nokama was just about to go back to the surface when her eyes caught something gleaming on the tunnel bottom. She dove down for a closer look.

It was a Rahi, quite dead, but not like anything she had seen before. Long and serpentlike, its body measured a good 65 feet in length by her estimation. Its tail was covered in spikes that measured a good three feet long. Even in death, it gave off an aura of amazing strength.

What was this creature? she thought as she swam rapidly for the transport. *And more importantly — what would have the power to kill it? Have we escaped the dangers of Metru Nui only to find something far worse?*

Whenua turned his head slowly back and forth, his Mask of Night Vision illuminating every corner of the tunnel. There had been no further sign of any monstrous Rahi, but that did nothing to ease his mind.

He knew he should share his suspicions about the two creatures, one living and one dead, encountered so far. But what if he was wrong? What if they were not the Rahi he remembered, and there was no connection to the project? Then he would not only have exposed one of the most closely guarded secrets in Onu-Metru, but he would have made a fool of himself in the process.

No. If I'm wrong, then my silence does no harm, he decided. *And if I'm right . . . I don't even want to think about that.*

The transport suddenly lurched with such violence that Whenua was almost thrown over the side. He turned to see Matau fighting the controls and the other Toa Metru scattered like fireflyer bugs in a stiff wind.

"What in Mata Nui's name are you trying to do?"

"We have to go back," Matau replied, as if it were the most obvious thing in the world. "We belong back in the city, doing our jobs. Hang on tight."

The transport lurched again as Matau tried to force it into a U-turn in too narrow a space. Whenua recognized the toneless quality of the Toa of Air's voice, as well as the undercurrent of conviction that he was absolutely doing the right thing. Whenua glanced up, the light from his mask playing across the ceiling. That's when he saw them.

"Vahki!" he shouted, pointing up. A squad of seven Nuurakh, the Ta-Metru order enforcers, were hovering just below the tunnel roof. Their Staffs of Command were deployed. One had already hit Matau with a blast, turning him into their obedient tool.

Nuju fired a stream of ice at Matau. In a flash, the Toa of Air's arms were pinned to his sides. That left the transport with no driver as it spun in rapid circles. Nokama ran, flipped, and landed beside Matau to take over the controls.

With no more reason to conceal themselves, the Vahki let loose with stun blasts. The Toa countered, Nuju using his elemental powers to create ice mirrors and reflect the energy bolts. Vakama tossed a spread of fireballs to give himself some cover. Then he rammed a low-powered Kanoka disk into his launcher and fired.

The disk struck one of the Vahki head-on, immediately triggering the disk's "reconstitutes at random" power. As Vakama hoped, it scrambled the clockwork mechanisms inside of the Vahki, sending the enforcer into an uncontrolled plunge beneath the waves.

Onewa reached out with his Mask of Mind Control, but being mechanical, Vahki minds were not vulnerable to the mask's energies. "Okay, we'll do it the hard way," said the Toa of Stone. Unleashing his elemental powers, he caused stone spikes to erupt from underwater, pinning three Vahki to the ceiling.

"Crude, but effective," said Nuju. "But can you do this?"

The Toa of Ice triggered his Mask of Telekinesis, tearing a huge chunk of stone from the ceiling. It slammed down onto a hovering Nuurakh, sending the Vahki spinning out of control. The mechanical being crashed into a wall and collapsed, its works shattered.

Matau had broken free of his icy bonds and was struggling with Nokama. Whenua lumbered over and grabbed the Toa of Air. "Go see your friends," he said, hurling Matau into the air.

The Toa crashed into the last two Vahki, stunning them both. Nokama maneuvered the transport underneath Matau and Whenua easily caught him as he fell. "There. This makes up for that time in the maintenance tunnels when you thought I let you fall," said the Toa of Earth. Then he turned to the other Toa and said, "Any idea what we do with the junior Vahki here?"

Onewa nodded. Then he triggered his mask power, reaching into the mind of Matau. As a crafter, he knew just when a hammer was needed and when a more delicate tool would get the job done. He carefully applied the mask-energies to drive out the Vahki's influence.

Matau shook his head like he had just awakened from a nap. "What happened? Why aren't we moving? And, um, why is Whenua carrying me?"

"We flipped a disk," said Onewa, "and he lost."

A small figure watched the Toa sail with a mixture of curiosity and fear in his eyes. He had never seen these Toa before. Who were they? Why were they here?

His expression grew grim, for he could already guess the answers to those questions. Their fight with the Vahki had not fooled him. These six, whoever they might be, must have been sent by the city of Metru Nui. And they could only have come on such a dangerous journey for one reason: to capture him. They might even intend harm for his friends.

Yes, of course. After all this time, no one had forgiven or forgotten. They were hunting him and the others again and would keep on doing so until they were stopped.

I just wanted to be left alone, he thought. *I didn't want to harm anyone. But they don't under- stand. No . . . it's not that they don't . . . they refuse to understand!*

He turned away and slipped into a narrow crevice, beginning the long journey home. Dark thoughts swirled in his brain, and from them a complex plan sprang.

I will make them understand, he vowed. *If I have to send their Toa back to them, crushed and de- feated, to do it . . . then so it will be.*

"Are you certain about this?" asked Nuju.

Nokama stood at the bow of their vessel, preparing to dive into the river. She had pulled Nuju aside a few moments before and whispered to him her intention of scouting ahead. Now the Toa of Ice looked at her with concern.

"I realize I am the last person you would expect to call for all of us to stay together," said

Nuju. "But we are facing completely unknown dangers here."

"You're absolutely right," Nokama replied. After a pause, she added, "You *are* the last person I would expect to suggest that. Are you sure you're Nuju, and not another shapeshifting Rahi?"

Nuju didn't crack a smile.

Nokama shrugged. "I won't be gone long. The others probably won't even notice. I just wanted someone to know, in case . . ."

"Yes," said Nuju. "In case."

Without another word, Nokama dove into the water and swam away. He stared after her for a long time.

Nokama plunged beneath the murky river. Although she did not have Whenua's night vision power, her eyes had become used to piercing the darkness underwater. She swam slowly, looking right and left for any sign of danger.

The river teemed with little fish and some larger predators, but nothing of a size that would threaten a Toa. They seemed more frightened of her than anything else. She had expected more of the monsters that had appeared earlier, but so far this waterway seemed about as dangerous as the Archives aquarium.

She surfaced to grab a breath of air. That was when she noticed the carvings in the wall of the tunnel. The action of the waters over time had worn them away to the point where they could not be read, so there was no way to be certain when they were made or why. But that still left the question — who had done this? Had someone else from Metru Nui made it through the Great Barrier in the past? Or did some other beings live in the world beyond, and this carving was their handiwork?

She went back beneath the surface, this time looking for other carvings. Instead, she spotted what looked like a loose rock in the wall. On closer examination, she found that the stone was not only loose, but it was not even a natural part of the wall. Its edges were smooth, as if it had been carved in Po-Metru. Another of the same was fitted on top of it, and another, and another.

Her eyes followed them up the side of wall to the ceiling. The rocks were holding a much larger slab in place, but if they were to become dislodged . . .

Someone rigged this, she realized. *Replaced the stones in the wall with these so that the slab could be brought down on anyone journeying this way. But why? And who knows how many other such traps there might be?*

She turned and swam as fast as she could toward the *Lhikan*. The other Toa had to be warned.

We are not alone here.

Nuju still stood, watching for Nokama. Now and then he would create a small shower of ice crystals and toss them into the water. She had been gone too long. He would give her a minute more and then tell the others they had to launch a search.

The transport lurched, swinging violently

to the right. Nuju turned and saw Matau angrily striking the wheel and muttering to himself.

"What's the matter?"

"It won't go!" growled Matau. "Everything is working, but it is not swim-speeding."

"Nokama understands watercraft better than any of us," said Vakama. "Where is she?"

"She went for a swim," Nuju replied. Before the others could question him further, he said, "I will dive and check. Perhaps we are snagged on something."

Nuju was not, in fact, that much bigger a fan of water than were Matau and Onewa. But he preferred a swim in the river to having to explain where Nokama had gone and why he had not informed the others. He wasn't sure himself why he had respected her wishes. But she had earned his respect, which was not an easy thing to do.

Below the boat, he found his diagnosis had been correct. A number of the legs that acted as oars were caught by some kind of seaweed. He used an ice dagger to cut some away and his Mask of Telekinesis to move a bit of the rest, but more always appeared. If he was going to clear the boat, he would need help.

He kicked hard to propel himself to the surface, only to find that he wasn't moving up, but down. The seaweed had wrapped itself around his legs and torso and was dragging him toward the bottom. He tried to aim his crystal spikes to freeze the vegetation, only to have his arms pinned to his sides by the growth. Before he could react, a stray strand had yanked off his mask. Weakness flooded his limbs as the Mask of Power drifted to the bottom.

Now he could see his final destination more clearly and the sight puzzled him. He knew his mind was cloudy due to the absence of the mask, but he could have sworn seaweed was a plant. Since when did it have huge jaws filled with knife-sharp teeth, gaping wide to devour a Toa?

Since now, he said to himself. *And weak as I am, there is no way I can stop it!*

Vakama watched the water with worried eyes. Nuju had been down there too long and Nokama was still not back. If something was waiting down below, going in to rescue the Toa of Ice might just lead to another Toa's disappearance. But the alternative was to stand and do nothing, something Vakama refused to do. He knew all too well the consequences of inaction in the face of danger.

The Toa of Fire had made up his mind to dive, when the vessel suddenly shot forward. His first reaction was relief. Nuju had obviously been successful and would be surfacing at any moment. This feeling faded in a hurry when he realized the boat was moving much too fast.

"Matau! Slow down!" he shouted.

The Toa of Air shook his head frantically. "I

can't! It's not the transport that is quick-floating, it's the current!"

A glance behind confirmed Matau's statement. The liquid protodermis flowing through the channel was now a raging torrent propelling the transport along. Onewa and Whenua hung on as the boat careened off the walls. Vakama fought to keep his balance as he made his way to the cockpit.

"Use your power!" he told Matau. "See if you can slow us down."

Matau leapt onto the bow of the vessel and used his Toa energies to call forth a windstorm. Gusts howled in the confined space, trying to force the boat back even as the current thrust it forward. Finally, the transport came to a halt, pinned between the two powerful forces.

It was a stalemate that could not last. Vakama barely heard Onewa shouting something over the roar of wind and wave. He turned to see the seals on the ship giving way and the outer shell fragmenting. Much more of this and there would be no transport left.

It never came to that. Matau staggered from the effort of maintaining the storm. The winds died down and the vessel began flying through the tunnel again. Vakama jumped into the cockpit and took the wheel.

"Onewa, grab Matau!" he barked. "Whenua, I need you to —"

The Toa of Earth wasn't listening. The archivist in him was looking with wonder at the river, whose current carried the boat along as if it were a toy. "It's incredible," he muttered. "This world never ceases to amaze me."

Vakama buzzed Whenua's mask with a luke-warm firebolt. "That's what you think," snapped the Toa of Fire. "It's going to cease in about three seconds if we don't think of something!"

Whenua turned. Looming before the transport was a massive whirlpool, more than large enough to swallow the boat and all its passengers. The *Lhikan* was dead on course for destruction.

Nokama had almost made it back to the transport when the current hit her. Being a native of

Ga-Metru, she had dealt with sudden undertow and freak tidal surges before. Before it could carry her too far, she dug her hydro blades into the rock walls to halt her progress. She was safe, but helpless to stop the *Lhikan* as it flashed past her.

The Toa of Water was not ready to give up. She focused her elemental energies on the river, trying to force the current to reverse, or at least slow enough that the others would be all right. But the current was too powerful and the transport already too far away for her to draw it back.

This is like trying to empty the silver sea with a test tube, she thought. *I should be able to master any natural tide . . . but what if this isn't natural? What if the same beings who rigged the traps up ahead are responsible for this too?*

Her thoughts were interrupted by a flash of white off to her right. It was followed by a wave of bitter cold that sent shivers through her frame. Either one by itself would have meant nothing, but together they made her instincts scream: *Nuju!*

The current was too strong to swim against.

Nokama pulled one of her hydro blades free and dug it back into the wall, then did the same with the other. It meant pulling herself along at a painfully slow pace. At one point, her hand slipped from her Toa tool and the current slammed her into the wall. She fought to stay conscious and hang on to the other blade. Letting go would mean being swept away.

Now a white object was shooting toward her through the water, followed swiftly by another. She couldn't tell what they were. She reached out as the first came near, grabbing it. It was Nuju's Mask of Power!

Now the larger object had almost reached her. With both hands full, she threw her body out at a 90 degree angle from the wall and scissored her legs to catch Nuju. His speed through the water threw her off balance and both Toa collided hard with the wall. Nokama winced as her right arm was wrenched. It took everything she had not to lose her grip and doom them both.

Without his mask, Nuju was so much dead weight. Nokama strained until she could fit the

Kanohi back on to the Toa of Ice. Nuju's eyes glowed brighter and he immediately grasped the situation. He grabbed one of the hydro blades and used his power to create a shell of ice around the two Toa.

"This will not last long," Nuju said. He coughed up some of the river water.

Nokama gestured at the strands of seaweed still wrapped around Nuju's arms. "What is that?"

"One of the river creatures wanted a cold meal," he replied. "The current changed its mind. Where are the others?"

Nokama shook her head. "Nuju . . . they're gone. I saw the transport go by, but I couldn't . . ."

Nuju put an arm around her. "Do not fear, Nokama. We will find them." *If they still exist to be found,* he added to himself.

"I have had enough," said Onewa. "We were branded criminals, captured, imprisoned, saw our friends taken by Makuta and our city damaged beyond repair. Now we are about to lose our lives and the lives of the only six Matoran we could save."

He turned to Whenua. "It stops now. And you are going to stop it."

Whenua's eyes were fixed on the whirlpool. Despite Vakama's best efforts in the cockpit, the transport was still headed right for it. "What are you talking about?"

"Just listen," said Onewa. "I have a plan."

Vakama had given up on hoping to avoid the whirlpool. Now he was trying to calculate the best way to ride with it and minimize the damage to the transport and Matoran spheres. If the craft shattered, maybe they could still salvage most, if not all, the spheres before they were lost.

Then he saw something rising from the water. Before his mind could even register what it was, the transport had struck the object and was flying through the air. The whirlpool passed beneath and then the transport dove, its momentum spent. It plunged bow first into the river, the water swamping the deck. The craft came close to capsizing before righting itself and bobbing back to the surface.

"What in Mata Nui's name just happened?" said Vakama. He was too surprised even to notice that the current had calmed and the boat was no longer rocketing forward.

"I did," Whenua answered, smiling broadly.

"We did," corrected Onewa.

"A little Toa power, and instant earth ramp — up and over we went," said Whenua.

"My idea, of course," broke in Onewa. "The hard part was explaining the plan in time to make it work. So —" He gently tapped the Great Mask of Mind Control he wore.

"You used the mask," said Vakama, hardly able to believe it. "You were directing his actions."

"His Toa power. My mind," replied Onewa. "An unbeatable combination. By the way, Whenua, your brain is as cluttered as your Archives. How do you manage to think?"

"I don't know," laughed Whenua. "I guess I

am just used to having more than one thought at a time, carver. You should try it."

"Then we're safe for now," said Vakama, not sounding as if he believed his own words. "We have to go back for Nokama and Nuju."

Onewa glanced behind and shook his head. "No, we don't. Look!"

In the distance, Nokama was heading their way using her hydro blades to pull her along. Above her, Nuju traveled via an ice bridge created with his Toa power. Both looked exhausted, but unharmed. They reached the *Lhikan* at the same time. Matau looked on, frowning, as Nuju helped Nokama onto the deck.

"It's good to see you both," said Vakama. "But how did you avoid the whirlpool?"

Nokama looked at the Toa of Fire as if he had lost his senses. "What whirlpool?"

Vakama rushed to the stern of the vessel. Sure enough, the waters were dead calm. There was no sign the maelstrom had ever been there. But it had been real, and so had the rushing water, the damage to the boat proved that.

He crouched down and stared into the water. The current had slowed and the whirlpool vanished just moments after the *Lhikan* would have been lost.

Almost as if someone was controlling them. Someone who wasn't close enough to see what happened, he thought. *Once they thought we had vanished into the whirlpool, there was no reason to continue it.*

He turned back to the others. "Someone tried very hard to kill us. Now that someone thinks we're all dead."

Whenua and Matau looked surprised. Onewa shrugged, no longer able to be shocked by anything that happened to the Toa Metru. Nokama and Nuju nodded in agreement.

"So what do we do about it, firespitter?" asked the Toa of Stone.

"That's simple," answered Vakama, rising to his feet. "We're going to die."

The *Lhikan* drifted aimlessly down the river. No Toa sat at the controls to keep it on course, nor was there anyone keeping watch for threats. In fact, there was no sign of life anywhere on the vessel.

To an observer, it would have appeared there had been a great struggle on board. One of Matau's aero slicers was embedded in the cockpit. Other parts of the craft were scarred by heat and ice blasts. The story was there for anyone to read: Some great force had overwhelmed the Toa Metru and swept them away, no doubt to their doom.

But if that observer's eyes had been able to see through the solid walls of the transport, quite a different tale would have unfolded before him. Six Toa Metru huddled inside the cramped hold, listening intently to the noises from outside.

"Do you hear anything?" Nokama whispered to Vakama.

The Toa of Fire shook his head, frustrated. He had been certain that if it appeared he and the others had been lost in the whirlpool, their mysterious foe would reveal himself. Of course, that assumed their enemy had some use for the ship and some need to confirm their deaths. If that wasn't the case, he could just leave the *Lhikan* to drift.

Onewa was saying something, but the words sounded like they were coming from far away. Vakama's mind had spun into another of his visions, brief glimpses of the future . . . or was it the past?

Monstrous Rahi, ancient when Metru Nui was young . . . driven from their home waters . . . jaws opened wide . . . tentacles reaching, reaching . . .

The craft spun, then lurched violently from side to side, shocking Vakama awake. They were no longer moving forward, he realized. They were going down!

Onewa sprang to his feet and tried the makeshift hatch, but it was stuck fast. They could all feel the change in pressure as the transport sank rapidly. Nokama used her power to summon an undersea wave to lift them back to the surface, but whatever force was pulling them down was too strong.

A crack appeared in the hull beside Nuju. River water began to leak slowly in, rapidly joined by other leaks in other portions of the hold. Already the liquid was up to the Toa's ankles and rising.

"Vakama, burn a hole in the hull," said Nokama. "We have to get out of here."

"If I do that, the *Lhikan* is lost," Vakama replied, "and so are the six Matoran spheres. There has to be another option!"

The transport shuddered violently as it struck the bottom of the waterway. The Toa Metru scrambled to hang onto something to keep from being slammed around the hold. The hull of the craft groaned as the increased water pressure threatened to cave it in.

"Don't look now, Toa of Fire," said Onewa. "But I think we just ran out of options."

The octopoid beast that held the *Lhikan* in its grasp carefully examined its catch. This strange thing did not belong here, so it had to be stopped. But now that the Rahi had the hard object, it was not sure what next to do. This thing did not live or breathe; it was not food; it had not even provided sport by trying to get away.

The Rahi's dim brain realized that this catch was of no use at all. Still, if allowed to escape, it might be an obstacle in the future. Better to avoid that by destroying it now.

The creature's tentacles began to squeeze the *Lhikan*, with enough force to shatter the ship to splinters. . . .

4

Mavrah stepped into the vast cavern, feeling a mixture of satisfaction and sadness. Given the choice, he would have preferred to simply scare those intruders away rather than harm them. But he knew enough about Toa to know they never gave up, not even in the face of overwhelming force. Certainly, Toa Lhikan had never flinched before any threat. Strange that he hadn't been among these strangers?

Still, it was good to know his inventive genius had not deserted him after all these years. The whirlpool had worked perfectly. Of course, he hadn't waited to see the intruders' boat wrecked by it. There would have been no joy in that.

For a moment, Mavrah was lost in his memories. He could remember long days spent in the Archives, talking with Nuparu about their newest ideas for inventions. Nuparu was determined to one day perfect a new mode of transport to replace chutes, if only to knock the Le-Matoran down a few pegs.

For his part, Mavrah had simply wanted to better understand the Rahi. It frustrated him that so many of the creatures had to be kept in stasis in the Archives, where little could be learned of them. How could a researcher study the behavior patterns of creatures who were always asleep? Sometimes he had fantasized about smashing open the stasis tubes just to see one of those magnficent Rahi move again.

Mavrah jumped as a great serpentlike creature snaked down from a stalactite and brushed against him. The Rahi was on its way to the water, a trip that would take some time given that the beast was over 40 feet long from head to tail. "Mustn't scare me like that," Mavrah said gently. "I might have thought it was another Toa, come to bring us all back."

The Onu-Matoran turned as two mechanized beasts entered from side passages. They took no notice of him, but instead took positions on either side of the serpent. They would make sure it got to the pool without incident and without being observed by any intruders. Where one group of Toa had come, more might follow.

Mavrah walked across the cave and stood at the edge of the vast pool. Beneath its calm surface lived countless creatures, remnants of an age long before Metru Nui. Powerful, unpredictable, dangerous beyond measure, they were still Mavrah's only friends in this desolate place. And no one — *no one* — would take them away from him.

One of those "friends" was busy at the moment trying to crack open the *Lhikan*. The octopoid Rahi had found the Vahki transport a tougher target than it expected, but it was only a matter of seconds before the hull gave way.

Suddenly, the transport began to glow red. An intense shock of searing heat forced the Rahi to let go, allowing the craft to bob back up to the surface.

Slowly, the glow faded. A few moments later, the hatch opened and the Toa Metru emerged on the deck. Vakama stumbled and almost fell before Nokama caught him. "Take it easy," she said.

"That was the hardest stunt I have ever had to pull," said Vakama. "So much heat without flame . . . but it worked."

"I wonder what it was that strong-pulled us down?" asked Matau. "And where is it now?"

A massive tentacle erupted out of the water, wrapping itself around Matau and hauling him off the transport. "When will I quick-learn to stop asking stupid questions?" shouted the Toa of Air, just before he disappeared beneath the waves.

As one, the Toa Metru dove in after him. A swipe of a tentacle sent Nuju flying through the water. A second tentacle grabbed Vakama. Nokama turned to rescue the Toa of Fire, but he waved her off.

In a moment, she saw why — or rather, she didn't see. Triggering the power of the Mask of Concealment, Vakama faded from view. The Rahi was puzzled. It could feel something in its grip, but not see anything. Its grip slackened just enough for Vakama to slip through, reappearing beside Onewa.

Matau was in bad shape. He hadn't been able to grab a breath of air before being pulled under and was rapidly drowning. Worse, the Rahi had started to swim away with its prey. Onewa glanced at Whenua, who nodded. Then both unleashed their elemental power, forming hands of earth and stone that reached up from the bottom to grab the creature.

Nuju rocketed forward, using both his elemental and mask energies. Bolts of ice and stone hurled telekinetically battered the beast. Stunned, it let go of Matau. Nokama caught him and rushed him to the surface.

Onewa and Whenua released the struggling Rahi and the creature swam away. Vakama gestured urgently for the Toa to head back to the transport.

They were still climbing aboard when the Toa of Fire shouted, "Matau! We need to go now!"

Nokama and Matau looked at him, surprised. But the Toa of Air could tell this was no time to argue. He leapt into the cockpit and started the craft moving forward.

"We are going after the beast," Nuju said to Vakama. It wasn't a question.

"Yes, we are," the Toa of Fire replied. "It's time we became the hunters."

From a hiding place nearby, six pairs of audio receptors recorded Vakama's words. Six pairs of optical sensors studied the Toa Metru, their strengths, their weaknesses, and their current condition. Complex clockwork mechanisms began to analyze, evaluate, and plan the ideal time to strike.

One of the six beings turned away and began the trek back home. In any conflict, defeat was an option. Logic dictated that the information gathered should therefore be relayed to others for future use if necessary. This unit would return to Mavrah to do just that while the others pursued and apprehended the intruders.

Had these beings possessed muscles, they would have felt them tense in anticipation of the conflict to come. If blood coursed through their veins, it would have flowed that much faster at the thought of battle after so many years of inactivity. But instead, they could only stare at the Toa with cold calculation. There would be no anger or hatred in their attack — just pure, precise, efficient destruction.

Nuju stood at the bow of the ship. The telescopic lense built into his Mask of Power was focused on the wake of the octopoid beast. Nokama stood beside him, prepared to continue the pursuit underwater if the creature chose to dive.

Near the cockpit, Vakama and Onewa strategized. Despite their disagreements, the two Toa had developed a grudging respect for each other. If Vakama still had his moments of doubt, and Onewa still thought with his mouth too often, they remained the best tacticians among the Toa. Whenua had been invited to join their council, but had refused, preferring to keep to himself.

All of the Toa turned at Nuju's cry. The river had opened up into a vast waterway, even wider than the Po-Metru Sculpture Fields. The Rahi they were chasing had vanished into its depths, but no one even noticed. Their eyes were on the dozens of monsters breaching the surface and bellowing their anger at the *Lhikan*.

Nokama had lived by the silver sea all her life. Between her explorations underwater and her visits to the Archives she had seen every kind of aquatic creature in existence, or so she believed. But never had she seen anything like this in the flesh. Before her startled eyes, serpents almost as long as the Coliseum was high reared up out of the water. Bizarre creatures looking like oversized sea slugs slithered along the rocky coastline. Massive fish leapt high into the air, lightning bolts lancing from their razor-sharp fins.

The sight of so many previously unknown Rahi was beautiful, in a way, but it was a savage beauty. To the right, a reptilian creature rose out of the water with a Tarakava squirming in its huge jaws. On the left, a Rahi much like the one the *Lhikan* had been chasing struggled helplessly in the grasp of two gigantic crablike creatures.

"This is . . . amazing," Nokama said softly.

"This is insane," replied Nuju.

"You're both wrong," said Whenua. "This . . . this is a disaster."

"Maybe we should quiet-sneak away, before they decide we are fish food," offered Matau.

Vakama shook his head. "No. We have nothing to turn back to — only a dark and dead city, filled with sleeping Matoran who are counting on us to find them a haven. If that means crossing these waters, then that is what we will do."

"I hate to say it, fire-spitter, but you're making a lot of sense," said Onewa.

"Why do you hate to say it?"

"Ruins my image," said the Toa of Stone.

Mavrah watched the mechanized Kralhi's approach. He knew it wouldn't have returned alone unless it had news, most likely bad news.

As a Matoran, it was hard for him to see the machine creature without a trace of fear. Long before the Vahki enforcers were put into operation in Metru Nui, the responsibility for law enforcement fell on the shoulders of the Kralhi. They were well-equipped for the task. Their stingerlike tails were capable of projecting a force bubble around a target. Once inside, the target was rapidly drained of energy, all of which was fed back into the Kralhi. This left whoever the Kralhi had captured far too weak to cause any trouble.

That, as it turned out, was the problem. The point had been to get Matoran troublemakers or those who walked off the job back to work as soon as possible. The Kralhi left them so weak and dizzy that they couldn't work for days. It was finally decided that they had to be shut down and replaced.

Saying that and doing it proved to be two very different things. To this day, no one was sure how much self-awareness the Kralhi might possess, but they certainly resisted being turned off and scrapped. The Matoran were successful with a few of them, but most fought back hard. With the help of the newly built Vahki, the Matoran achieved a victory of sorts by driving the Kralhi out of the city. No one knew, or cared, where they had disappeared to as long as they were gone.

Mavrah had been terrified the day he stumbled upon them, sure they would attack and force him back to the city. But the Kralhi had made no threatening moves. Over time, Mavrah realized that their primary purpose — to serve and protect Matoran — was still in force. As long as he did not make any effort to harm them or turn them off, they were perfectly willing to accept and serve him.

Now the Kralhi paused in front of him. When it spoke, it was with the recorded voice of one of the Toa: "It's time we became the hunters." Then the machine waited for a response.

Mavrah hesitated. He had tried to destroy these Toa and had been sure he succeeded. If they still lived, then it must be Mata Nui's will that they do so. Mavrah wondered if it was a sign. Perhaps if he explained to the Toa why he was here, and why he had to stay, they would understand.

Then they could return to Metru Nui and inform Turaga Dume to call off the search.

"Return," Mavrah ordered the Kralhi. "Capture the six Toa and bring them back here alive."

The Kralhi simply stared, as if it had not understood anything that was said. Mavrah knew the creature was just being willful and stubborn.

"Alive," he repeated, firmly. "Unharmed. That is a direct command. Now go."

The Kralhi turned and departed. Mavrah thought he detected something in the way it moved, but he dismissed the idea. *A Kralhi is just a machine*, he reminded himself. *It can't feel disappointment . . . can it?*

Unfortunately, not everything shared Mavrah's newfound desire for the Toa's safety. The *Lhikan* had made it about halfway across the lake before attracting the attention of the local wildlife. Now the beasts were shoving each other aside in a race to see who would get to devour the craft and occupants first.

The Toa had acquired one ally, a massive, tentacled whale that was now running interference for them. Onewa's Mask of Mind Control had worked on Rahi before, and this one had just enough of a mind to give him something to manipulate. Unfortunately, it meant the Toa of Stone could do nothing else to help to defend the vessel, but the others did their best to pick up the slack.

A horned serpent wrapped itself around the hull of the boat. Its head swung up over the side of the deck, hissing at Nuju and baring its vicious fangs. The Toa of Ice muttered, "No, I don't think so," and sent twin frigid blasts from his crystal spikes. Frozen solid, the serpent sank to the bottom like a stone.

On the other side of the vessel, entire schools of fish were launching themselves out of the water at the *Lhikan*. Matau had been using his elemental wind power to blow them away, until an inspiration struck him. Using the power of his Mask of Illusion, he transformed himself into a huge sharklike beast with three sets of jaws.

Frightened, the schools dove back underwater, with the exception of one fish who landed on the deck.

Matau glanced down at it. He had never been fond of marine life, and this was a particularly ugly specimen. *Has the same happy-smile as Makuta*, he thought. *Just what the world needs — a Makuta fish.*

Vakama was everywhere at once. Sea creatures, no matter how large, hated fire, and he had been able to drive away some of the more monstrous specimens. Those he could not stop were being battered by waves or grabbed by the sea bottom thanks to the powers of Nokama and Whenua. It seemed like the Toa might make it through, although Vakama wondered how they would ever be able to make a second trip this way with all the sleeping Matoran in tow.

A huge wave swamped the vessel, almost washing Vakama into the lake. When it subsided, all of the Toa could feel that something was wrong. The craft was still afloat, but now listing badly to one side.

"One of the spheres," Nokama said. "They must have taken one of the spheres! I have to go down there and —"

"No!" Nuju grabbed her and kept her from diving. "I let you go once, not this time. You would not last more than a few seconds among these creatures, and you know it. If one of the spheres has been lost, we will recover it . . ."

"When?" Nokama demanded. "Before or after some sea monster has dined on it?"

"I know how you feel," said Whenua, as he caused chunks of the sea floor to pelt an on-coming Rahi. "Believe me. But we are almost to the other side of the lake. Once back in the tun-nel, the creatures can only come at us one at a time. One Toa can hold them off while the rest of us —"

"That will be too late!" said Nokama, wrenching free of Nuju's grasp. She raced to the edge of the deck.

Vakama saw her and moved just as quickly himself. He threw up a wall of flame around the transport, cutting off the Rahi from approaching and Nokama from leaving. She turned on him, enraged.

"Vakama, why —?"

"We may have lost a friend," said the Toa of Fire. "I won't stand by while we lose another."

Before Nokama could answer, she was suddenly lifted off her feet and into the air. Vakama looked at Nuju, thinking it was the Mask of Telekinesis at work, but the Toa of Ice was as surprised as anyone. That was when Matau noticed the energy bubble around Nokama. He struggled to see through the flames, finally spotting what he feared to find but knew had to be there.

"Kralhi!" he shouted. "They have Nokama!"

"Whenua, you and Onewa keep the Rahi at bay," ordered Vakama. "Nuju, Matau and I will save Nokama!"

But Matau was already gone, encased in a Kralhi bubble and being spirited away. Nuju created an ice barrier to try and impede the bubble's progress, but a boulder hurled by the Kralhi weakened it badly. When Matau's prison struck it, the wall crumbled into the water.

Now the Kralhi attacked in earnest, keeping the Toa off balance with a barrage of stones and energy bubbles. Onewa was the next to be captured, causing the Rahi he had mastered to dive beneath the water and disappear.

The Toa fought valiantly, but attacked on two fronts and worn down with fatigue, they could not hold their own. Nuju had a perfectly aimed ice blast ready for a Kralhi when one of the Rahi rammed the transport, knocking him off his feet. The next instant, he was inside a Kralhi bubble and could feel his energy being drained away.

Vakama and Whenua held out for a little longer, but eventually they too fell to the Kralhi. Vakama screamed with anger and frustration as he saw the now abandoned transport drifting toward the tunnel, still carrying its precious cargo. Then the hunger of the Kralhi for energy took its toll. Vakama's mind fell into a pool of darkness as unconsciousness claimed them all.

5

Nuju had not expected to awaken. If he ever did see the light again, he assumed it would be from inside a cell, or at least with the Toa in chains. But the reality proved to be very different.

The first thing he saw when his eyes opened was the ceiling of a vast cavern. It was warm here, as if molten protodermis flowed underground to provide heat in the way it did in Metru Nui homes. He glanced around, trying not to move his head and give away that he was awake. He could see the other Toa, some stirring, some still unconscious. They were all lying on a comfortable bed of dried seaweed.

He might have thought the whole thing was a bad dream if not for the presence of three Kralhi, obviously standing guard. Realizing they could not be fooled, he sat up. His mechanical parts were undamaged, but his biological components ached badly. It would take time to recover from the Kralhi's energy drain.

The other Toa were now fully awake. Vakama started to get to his feet, but as soon as he did so, one of the Kralhi took a step forward. When the Toa of Fire sat back down, the guardian returned to its original spot.

"I guess we won't be going for any walks," said Onewa. "Kralhi. I never expected to see those junk heaps again."

"I say as soon as we are back to full strength, we make a run for the water and try to find the transport," said Nokama. "I didn't like those things when they patrolled Metru Nui. I like them even less here."

Vakama looked around. Amphibious Rahi of enormous size crawled and slithered around the cave, but they all stayed well away from the Kralhi. It made no sense. Why would these creatures fear and obey mechanical beings, and why would the Kralhi wish to control Rahi in the first place? What were they even doing here?

Whenua spotted a small figure coming

toward them from the other end of the cave. Walking by his side was a medium-sized Rahi that looked like a cross between a lizard and a Kavinika, wolflike creatures from Po-Metru. The Toa of Earth paid little attention to the beast, though — his eyes were focused on the too familiar Matoran approaching.

"You mustn't let my friends worry you," Mavrah said as he got closer. "They are just here to make sure you remain . . . reasonable."

"We're always reasonable," Onewa shot back. "In fact, I can think of a bunch of reasons to turn you into a rock garden."

Nokama gestured for Onewa to keep silent, and said, "Who are you? Why have you brought us here? You have to let us go. Our mission is vital!"

Mavrah chuckled. "Who am I? As if you don't know? I am aware of your mission, Toa — if that is what you really are. It is why I brought you here."

Onewa reached out with his Mask of Mind Control powers and seized hold of Mavrah's thoughts. The Matoran stiffened, then said exactly what Onewa wished him to: "Then again, you are correct. I will set you free. The Kralhi will escort you out."

The Rahi at Mavrah's side began to screech so loudly Onewa thought his mask would split. The Kralhi responded by launching weakness disks at each of the Toa. The power of the disk was enough to break Onewa's concentration and free Mavrah's mind.

The Matoran shook his head as if waking up from a bad dream. "You . . . you mustn't do that again. My pet here is a most unusual Rahi, you see. He can sense the use of Kanohi mask powers, in the same way a Kinloka rat can sense food from a distance. And, as you have now discovered, my Kralhi are very well trained."

The Matoran smiled. "Now, let us not waste time. My Rahi recovered your transport, yes, and those shiny spheres too . . . most remarkable creations. I am prepared to return them to you if you turn around, go back the way you came, and deliver a message to Turaga Dume for me."

"That might be . . . difficult," Vakama replied. "But what's the message?"

"Tell him to leave me alone!" Mavrah yelled, startling the Toa. There was an uncomfortable silence while the Matoran composed himself. Then he added, quietly, "I am fine. The Rahi are fine. We want nothing from Metru Nui, and Metru Nui should ask nothing of us."

The Toa glanced at each other, none of them eager to be the one to tell the Matoran about the fate of Metru Nui. Finally, Whenua stood up. The Kralhi advanced automatically, but the Toa of Earth ignored them.

"Mavrah, in Mata Nui's name . . . stop this," he said. The other Toa looked at him, shocked. Whenua knew this crazy Matoran?

Whenua took a step toward Mavrah, then another. The Matoran waved the Kralhi off. "You are fighting a battle long over, against enemies that no longer exist," the Toa of Earth continued.

"Metru Nui is no threat to you, my old friend, because Metru Nui is no more."

Mavrah said nothing as Whenua told his tale. He related the story of the Morbuzakh's attacks on the city; the transformation of six Matoran into Toa Metru; the betrayal of the false Dume; and the deathlike sleep of all the Matoran. When he was finished, he waited for the Matoran's reaction.

It wasn't long in coming, nor was it what Whenua had expected: Mavrah burst out laughing. "Lies," he said. "But amusing ones. Lhikan dropping off Toa stones like they were Naming Day gifts? Whenua, of all Matoran, a Toa? And Turaga Dume . . . oh, *forgive me*, Makuta . . . as sinister mastermind? Yes, very funny indeed."

Mavrah's expression suddenly darkened. "The Whenua I knew was many things, but he was not a liar. That means you are not Whenua. I cannot trust you, any of you."

The Kralhi advanced until they were crowding the Toa against the cavern wall. Mavrah came with them, his eyes fixed on Whenua. "I know there is no cell that could hold true Toa. But I am guessing that your ship means something to you or you would not have fought so hard to save it. Make a move to escape, or to harm me, and I will see it destroyed, along with those strange spheres. I want no trouble from the six of you —"

Mavrah stopped abruptly. The Rahi by his side had begun to screech again. He examined the five Toa before him, and . . . five? He was sure there had been six of them. Yes, there had been six, which meant —

"One of them has escaped!" he shouted. He gestured toward two Kralhi emerging from the shadows on the far side of the cave. "Find him! Bring him back!"

The mechanical beasts turned and exited through a side tunnel. Nokama watched them go, nursing a hope that Vakama would manage to escape and find the transport. His Mask of Concealment had allowed him to fade from view while Mavrah was talking. The Matoran had been so upset he never noticed the shadow Vakama still cast even while invisible.

Mata Nui, if you can hear me, help Vakama, she thought. *The fate of all Matoran rests with him now.*

The Kralhi began their hunt, moving slowly and methodically through the only tunnel the stranger would logically have taken. His invisibility was at best an annoyance to them. Their more sophisticated sensors would surely be able to track him.

Still, it was more than their absolute confidence in victory that added an intangible sense of excitement to this pursuit. It was something very simple, yet with potentially horrific consequences for the Toa of Fire: Mavrah had not said this one needed to be brought back alive.

Vakama moved as quickly as he could. The problem with invisibility, he had discovered, was that he could not see himself either. It was no easy trick to run when he couldn't see his feet.

He could hear the heavy footsteps of the Kralhi behind him. He had no idea if they would be able to see him or not, but was willing to gamble on the power of his Kanohi mask.

Vakama had only one Kanoka disk left, a freeze disk of fairly substantial power. A plan started to form in his mind. One disk would be more than enough, if he used it correctly . . .

He raced on, fitting the Kanoka in his launcher. Once he found the right spot for an ambush, the Kralhi were in for a big surprise.

Matau eyed the Kralhi guarding them. The three of them were standing like statues, but he knew that they were primed to react to any movement. He silently calculated just what combination of flips and rolls it would take to get close to them. All he asked was the chance to put his aero slicers to work.

"How long do we wait?" he whispered.

"We give Vakama ten minutes," Onewa replied. "Then we move. Nuju, Whenua and I will distract the Kralhi. You and Nokama will grab Mavrah."

"I never liked Onu-Matoran," muttered the Toa of Ice. "I like them even less now."

"Don't blame him. You don't understand," said Whenua.

"There's a lot we don't understand," Onewa shot back. "But I have a feeling you do. Maybe it's time you shared?"

Whenua hesitated for a long moment. Then he nodded and began to speak.

Whenua's Tale

Long before the Morbuzakh, long before the actions of the false Dumse, long before the coming of the Toa Metru, the city of Metru Nui was a place of peace and learning. Outside of the city-wide akilini tournaments in the Coliseum, the only real excitement was when Rahi beasts would appear on the outskirts. Then Toa Lhikan and the Vahki squads would go into action, driving off the creatures or trapping them for display in the Archives.

Being an experienced archivist, it was not unusual for Whenua's day to begin with news of the latest captures. But on this particular day, the pounding on his door was more frantic. He went to open it, mouthing a silent wish that no exhibits had broken free and trashed an entire wing again.

Onepu didn't even wait for the door to be

fully ajar before slipping inside. His eyes were bright with excitement and his heartlight was flashing wildly. "It's amazing! You have to come see! No one knows, not even Toa Lhikan!"

"Slow down," said Whenua. "You're talking faster than a Le-Matoran. Come see what? Were more Rahi delivered? Or did the miners find more of those Bohrok things?"

"Better than that. But I can't explain. The Chief Archivist wants you, me, and Mavrah there right away."

Onepu dashed back outside, with a confused Whenua following along behind. The last time the Chief Archivist wanted to see him, a few dozen ice bats had escaped from their tubes and infested the administrative offices. He hoped this time the meeting would not involve nets, boxes, or anything that flew.

The trip took longer than Whenua expected. Onepu led him on a winding path to the Archives, through chutes that dove deep beneath the surface and emerged in sub-levels with which

Whenua was only barely familiar. Then it was a long hike through abandoned tunnels to another chute, this one badly in need of repair, and another steep drop to a sub-level that didn't even show up on any Archives charts.

"Where are we?"

"Come on," said Onepu. "Wait until you see this."

The two Matoran rounded a corner to behold a stunning sight. This sub-level consisted almost completely of water, and in that water were creatures out of an archivist's dream . . . or nightmare. There were huge, aquatic beasts, large enough to swallow a Muaka in one gulp. Nearby were monstrous crabs strong enough to crush stone in their claws. The sight of one such Rahi would have been shocking, but there were dozens and dozens of them here.

Whenua did not know what to say. Onepu simply smiled. Mavrah was already there, just staring at the amazing display before him.

"I told you," said Onepu. "Even the Chief Archivist was speechless."

"Where did they come from?" asked Whenua. "What . . . what are they?"

Mavrah turned at the sound of voices. "They appeared off the coast of Onu-Metru last night," he said. "It took Mata Nui knows how many Vahki squads to herd them in here. This was the only spot in the city big enough to hold them all."

Whenua watched as one of the creatures surfaced long enough to reveal a Takea shark trapped in its jaws. Then it dove again, leaving little doubt what the fate of that unlucky sea beast would be.

"There isn't a stasis tube big enough in all of —" Whenua began.

"They aren't for exhibit." The three archivists turned to see Turaga Dume coming toward them. "The Chief Archivist has requested, and I have granted, permission for these creatures to be kept here for study. They will not be placed in stasis so that the three of you can learn from conscious specimens."

All three of them thanked the Turaga. Dume waved them off. "Don't thank me. This is against my better judgment. Unleashed, creatures like these could destroy half the city. For that reason, this matter is to be kept a strict secret. I do not want a panic in the city, do you understand?"

The archivists nodded. Never before had the Turaga knowingly allowed a danger to the city to exist within its borders. It was a little frightening to realize that not only the safety of the Archives, but perhaps Metru Nui itself, depended on how well they did their jobs.

"What about Toa Lhikan?" asked Whenua. "Surely he must know."

"No," answered Dume. "Lhikan's first duty is to the safety of the city, and he cannot see beyond that. But the advancement of Matoran science requires risk. I have been convinced that there is something that can be learned from these . . . monsters. Do not prove me wrong."

A serpent that looked roughly the size of Po-Metru raised its head above the water and bellowed. The sound shook the sub-level.

"And Mata Nui protect us all," said Dume as he walked away.

*　　*　　*

The three Onu-Matoran soon settled into a routine. Early each morning, they would travel together to the Archives. Staying in each others' company helped them avoid talking with any other archivists who might be curious about their new project. They spent all day and most of the night observing and testing the strange sea creatures, noting down everything they could about the behavior and characteristics of the Rahi. Then they would return to their homes for an all too brief rest before starting all over again.

Whenua and Onepu complained early and often that three Matoran were not enough to do this job well. But Mavrah insisted that secrecy was vital to the success of the project, and the Chief Archivist backed him up.

Fatigue and overwork eventually took their toll. The three Matoran began to quarrel over the slightest thing. Notes were misplaced, experiments accidentally ruined, and at one point one of the Rahi almost slipped past both Onepu and a Vahki squad to make it back out to sea.

That was enough to drive Mavrah to fury. "You idiot!" he shouted at Onepu. "Do you realize what might have happened if it escaped?"

"He's right," Whenua said. "It might have turned toward the city and harmed Matoran before it was stopped."

"Before it was stopped?" Mavrah repeated in disbelief. "Before it was killed, you mean, along with our entire project. Your stupidity could have led to this Rahi's destruction, a tragic loss to science — all because you weren't paying attention!"

It took some time for the hard feelings left over from that incident to ease. But worse was yet to come, and this time on Whenua's watch. He had been concentrating intensely on a creature that looked something like a Tarakava, only with multiple flippers that might evolve into feet one day. Though not big enough to be a physical threat to its neighbors, it was able to defend itself quite well with the help of twin ice beams from its eyes.

The Rahi was so fascinating that Whenua never saw a far larger beast erupt out of the water. Other creatures immediately moved to challenge it, but the monstrous serpent shrugged them off as if they were raindrops. It was sick of captivity. Now was the time to escape or die trying.

The monster leapt out of the water and crashed into the stone ceiling. The impact violently shook the Archives, sending Whenua plunging into the makeshift holding tank. Before he could scramble back to safety, the Rahi struck again. This time the force of the collision cracked the ceiling and shattered displays even on the uppermost levels.

Whenua had his own problems at the moment. He was *not* a strong swimmer. Worse, his neighbors in the water had noticed a newcomer in their midst, one with no claws or teeth to defend himself. This would be an easy meal, they decided, and began to circle the Matoran.

The archivist desperately tried to remember anything he had ever heard about fending off sea Rahi attacks. In a panic, he realized it was a subject he had never discussed. Onu-Matoran didn't go for swims, after all. Only Ga-Matoran were that insane.

One squid like Rahi reached out with its tentacle. Whenua frantically slapped it away. But he could already feel his arms and legs growing tired from treading water. He would run out of energy long before the Rahi ran out of interest. Then he would be just another archivist lost in the pursuit of knowledge.

A shark moved in for the kill. Too tired to fight anymore, Whenua shut his eyes and waited for the end. But instead of a painful bite, he felt hands seize him and pull him out of the water. A second later, he was back on solid ground, coughing and gasping for air.

Mavrah stood over him. "What were you thinking, diving in there?"

"I decided I needed a bath," Whenua snapped. "You think it was my choice to be Rahi bait? The earth tremors knocked me in."

"Those weren't tremors," Mavrah responded grimly. "One of our guests tried to escape. It's under control now, but . . . there was a lot of damage up above. A Kraawa broke free."

Whenua winced. The Kraawa was an unusual Rahi who turned any force used against it into energy to grow. Hit it enough times and it would be bigger than the Coliseum. Getting it into the Archives had taken multiple Vahki squads and resulted in three levels being trashed. If it was loose . . .

"How bad?" he asked.

"A dozen Vahki smashed; three levels suffered critical damage, four more are being evacuated; at least a few hundred exhibits awake and on the loose. It's a disaster."

"You have a gift for understatement, Mavrah."

The words came from Turaga Dume. The elder was striding toward them, with the Chief Archivist running alongside, babbling apologies. Dume waved him away and looked directly at Mavrah.

"This project is terminated," he said. "As soon as order has been restored in the Archives, the Vahki will drive these . . . these monsters back out of the city. A security zone will be established in the waters around Metru Nui. The Vahki have authorization to kill any of these Rahi who violates that zone."

"No!" Mavrah shouted. "You mustn't do that! Think of the knowledge we will be losing, the potential for progress —"

"This is not a debate," Turaga Dume replied. Then, in a softer tone, he added, "I am sorry, Mavrah. I know how much this project means to you. But I cannot jeopardize the safety of the Archives — or the city — further. These things do not belong here."

Dume turned to the Chief Archivist. "See to it that the Vahki get any cooperation they require. I want these beasts gone by morning."

That night was the longest Whenua had ever lived through. He couldn't help thinking that if he had been paying more attention, maybe this would never have happened. Of course, he couldn't say how he would have stopped a massive Rahi who wanted out, but that was beside the point. Now the Archives were half-wrecked and the project was shut down.

He had tried to apologize to Mavrah for his mistake, but the Onu-Matoran was too upset to speak. He just stood there, staring at the Rahi, looking like he had lost his best friends.

The next morning, Whenua returned to find the Archives under lock down. Vahki Rorzakh were everywhere, watching carefully as Onu-Matoran crews struggled to return Rahi to their stasis tubes. Inside, other crews used regeneration disks to repair structural damage. The sheer magnitude of the damage was staggering.

He made his way down to the sub-level where the Rahi had been held. He expected to find it abandoned. Instead, it was filled with Rorzakh and a very worried Chief Archivist.

"They're gone," the administrator said. "All of them. Disappeared."

"Wasn't that the point?" Whenua asked.

"You don't understand. The Rahi are gone, but the Vahki didn't take them. They escaped back to sea somehow. The Vahki are bringing Onepu and Mavrah here now."

A Rorzakh squad appeared a moment later, shoving Onepu in front of them. A second squad was right on their heels, but empty-handed.

"Where's Mavrah?" asked the Chief Archivist.

The Vahki shrugged. Whenua had no doubt they had searched Mavrah's home and everywhere he might be hiding before returning to admit failure. Rorzakh were nothing if not thorough.

"He must be on his way then," the Chief Archivist muttered, not sounding at all convinced that was the case. "I have already spoken with the Turaga. He is sending Bordakh and Rorzakh to find the creatures. Of course, the important thing is that they are gone. But I think we all want to find out how and why."

Whenua said nothing. But he had a horrible suspicion he already knew the answers to those questions . . .

The mystery of the missing Rahi was never solved. The Chief Archivist's official report to the Turaga stated that the creatures must have contrived a mass escape. The Vahki on duty had done nothing to prevent it because their orders were

to see to it that the Rahi left. It made no difference to them how that happened.

The report further stated that, in trying to
stop the escape, Mavrah had been lost and was
presumed dead. Although his sacrifice could not
be publicly recognized without revealing the
existence of the project, the sub-level would be
renamed in his honor.

Whenua always suspected that Turaga
Dume knew more about what had happened
than he let on. He called off the Vahki search for
the Rahi after only a very short time, as if he
knew they would not be found, nor would
Mavrah. Whatever the Rorzakh knew about the
situation, they communicated only to the Turaga.

After a while, things returned to normal in
the Archives. Whenua and Onepu both made an
effort to forget all that had gone on. It was easier
to simply accept the official report and mourn
for their friend. After all, the only alternative the-
ory of what happened that night was too far-
fetched to ever believe.

Or so they thought . . .

"But Mavrah wasn't dead," Nokama said slowly, still trying to comprehend what she had just heard. "He stole the Rahi somehow before the Vahki could move them."

"Then wound up here, where he stumbled on the Kralhi," Onewa continued. "It's a community of outcasts."

Nuju turned to Whenua, saying, "You knew all along. When we first encountered the beasts, you knew what they had to be."

"I wasn't sure," said the Toa of Earth. "And . . . Mavrah saved my life. And he wouldn't be here if it weren't because of me — my mistake."

"What's done is done," said Nokama. "But I think we should make a pact: In the future, no more secrets."

Onewa chuckled. "Well, we know who the

most optimistic Toa is," he said. "But it's the absent one who concerns me. Where in Mata Nui's name is Vakama?"

The Toa of Fire was asking himself the same question. He had taken so many twists and turns he was not at all sure he could find his way back to the other Toa. But he had found a perfect spot to trap the two Kralhi on his trail.

Now he was perched on a rocky ledge that afforded him a decent view of the tunnel. He would have to wait for both of them to approach before he could act, and then strike the rearmost machine first. The problem was by then they would be able to sense him too. Vakama held his breath and did his best to remain motionless.

The sound of the Kralhi's footfalls grew louder and louder. A moment later, both of them came into view, walking in single file in the narrow tunnel. Vakama forced himself to wait for just the right instant.

The lead Kralhi lifted its head, looking in his direction. Had it spotted him? There was no more time to delay. Vakama launched the freeze disk at the Kralhi in the rear at the same as he hurled a blast of elemental fire at the lead machine.

Ice and fire hit at the same time. The intense heat fused the components of the lead Kralhi, destroying its control centers. The Kanoka disk froze the other solid before it could react. The damaged Kralhi, its sensors blinded, stumbled backwards and smashed into its partner, shattering the second enforcer into a million icy fragments. Then it collapsed on the floor in a heap, sparks flying from its joints.

Vakama dove from his hiding place and ran down the tunnel. Even at top speed, he barely made it clear before the Kralhi exploded.

That should show Mavrah what I — what a Toa — can do, he corrected himself. *If he has any sense, he'll surrender right now. Next time, I might not be quite so gentle.*

Vakama ran on. Now free of pursuit, he no longer bothered to remain invisible. A few small cave Rahi eyed him as he passed by, but none of them posed any threat. He did not even notice them. His mind was fixed on one thought: find the transport.

Mata Nui must have been smiling upon him, for as he rounded a bend, he spotted the battered hulk of the *Lhikan*. It was beached in a small cove, resting lopsidedly on some rocks. The reason for that was frighteningly clear. Nokama had been right, one of the spheres was missing.

Where is it? Vakama wondered grief-stricken. *Which Matoran has been lost, and how will we ever find him?*

A lone silver sphere rested at the bottom of the lake. Monstrous Rahi swam around and above it, yet none dared to approach too closely. It was a dead thing, true, but it did not seem like food. One hungry fish had already shattered its teeth trying to take a chunk out of the object.

Inside the sphere, the Po-Matoran named Ahkmou lay in unending sleep. His dreams were filled with Morbuzakh vines, four-legged monsters backed by hulking brutes, Vahki squads, and

Great Disks. He had no idea where he was or why. His last memory was of sitting in the Coliseum and feeling a great weakness overcome him. Strangely enough, for a Matoran who had tried to betray the Toa Metru and the city, his final conscious thoughts had been: Where are the Toa? Why are they not here to save me?

Safe in his sphere, Ahkmou slept on, awaiting a being of power that would awaken him someday . . .

"Wake up!" Onewa shouted.

The sound shocked Whenua out of his own thoughts and back to the situation at hand. The explosion had distracted the Kralhi for an instant, long enough for the Toa Metru to make a move. Now Onewa was struggling with a Kralhi's tail, trying to keep it aimed away from his friends.

"I could use some help here!" said the Toa of Stone.

Whenua shook off his worries and grabbed hold of the mechanical monstrosity. The Kralhi was straining to turn itself so it could hook the

Toa with its tools. Onewa waited until he was sure Whenua had a good grip, then let go.

"Hold him steady," he said, "and be ready to jump!"

The Toa of Stone focused his elemental energies at the stone floor beneath the Kralhi's feet. At his command, the rock split apart, opening a crevice into which the Kralhi fell. Whenua barely let go in time, stumbling back from the edge of the gap.

"Now what?" asked the Toa of Earth. "He will just climb out again."

"No. I don't think so," Onewa replied.

The sides of the crevice suddenly slammed shut. Then they slowly opened again, to reveal a sparking, partially mangled machine. Then the front and back walls of the crevice did the same, compacting the Kralhi into a perfectly square block of cables and machinery.

"There," said the Toa of Stone. "As a mechanized guard, he makes a good brick."

On the other side of the cave, Nuju was leaping and dodging to stay out of the way of

Kralhi energy bubbles. He considered making a break for the tunnel, but thought better of it. The Kralhi would probably just let him go and turn its attention to Nokama and Matau. No, he would have to stand and fight.

Even as his body twisted and turned to avoid the energy-sapping spheres, Nuju's mind raced. The bubbles were incredibly powerful, generated from energy within the Kralhi. That opened some intriguing possibilities, provided he could keep the Kralhi focused on what was happening now and not what was about to happen.

"They laugh at you in Ko-Metru, you know," he said. "They call you 'Nuparu's folly.'"

The Kralhi moved in closer, launching energy bubbles at a rapid pace.

"We needed law enforcers," Nuju continued, ducking and dodging. "Instead, we got dusty, clanking energy vampires. They should have just sent all of you to the Moto-Hub and turned you into Ussal carts."

There was no way to know if the Kralhi understood the words, but it certainly caught the tone. In the old days, Matoran who spoke this way to a Kralhi would have been sapped of strength almost to the point of nonexistence. Order had to be maintained; insolence had to be punished.

"Or perhaps some furniture," the Toa of Ice taunted. "We could have broken you down for tables and chairs. Think of the market there would have been for genuine Kralhi footstools and ornament shelves."

The Kralhi's tail adjusted and locked on to Nuju. The end of it began to crackle as another energy bubble formed. Nuju turned and tried to run as if he were afraid, but, in fact, he was headed for a solid wall. Timing his moves to the split second, the Toa of Ice ran three-quarters of the way up the wall and turned the move into a backward flip. In mid-air, he launched ice blasts from both his crystal spikes.

His power met the Kralhi energies at their peak. A double-thick coating of solid ice encased the end of the machine's tail just as the energy bubble was about to launch. Now cut off from release, the massive energies of the Kralhi had nowhere to go but back upon itself.

Nuju hit the floor hard as the Kralhi began to shudder. The Toa used his powers to form a sphere of hard ice around himself. He finished it barely in time, as the feedback sparked a violent explosion that sent Kralhi parts flying everywhere. Nuju's sphere was blown backward and shattered against the stone wall.

The Toa of Ice lay stunned for a moment amidst shards of his protective sphere and white-hot Kralhi fragments. Then he slowly dragged himself to his feet and looked at the smoking ruin that a moment before had been a powerful robotic guardian.

"That's the problem with machines," he muttered. "They never think about the future."

Matau and Nokama had gotten the easy job. A simple wall of wind was enough to keep Mavrah's Rahi pet at bay, while Nokama firmly but gently pinned Mavrah against the wall. She had no wish harm the Matoran, just talk some sense to into him.

"We are not your enemies," she said, urgency in her voice. "Call off the Kralhi and talk with us. I know what happened, Mavrah, and why you left Metru Nui. But you don't have to stay here. You can come with us."

The Matoran struggled to break free. "Go with you where?" he said. "If you are telling the truth and Metru Nui is lost, there is nowhere to go. There is nothing beyond the river but death."

Nokama started to speak, then paused. For all she knew, Mavrah was right. They had only Vakama's vision to tell them that the way to safety was through the Great Barrier. What if he had been wrong? What if there was no haven for the Matoran?

Mavrah glanced over Nokama's right shoulder. She turned in time to see a Kralhi's forearm swinging at her. Too late to dodge, she rode with the blow as it flung her across the cave. Mavrah rushed to the water's edge.

"My friends! Hear me!" he shouted to the creatures in the lake. "The time has come to fight for your freedom!"

Nokama shook her head, not quite believing what she was seeing. The waters were churning as a horde of giant sea Rahi turned and began heading toward the cave. The other Toa saw it too, and were no less stunned.

"Those Rahi aren't listening to him, are they?" asked Onewa.

"Of course not," Nuju replied. "No one can command Rahi."

"Brothers! A little quick-help!"

They turned to see Matau trapped between two Kralhi. The Toa of Air had summoned a windstorm, but the Kralhi were too heavy to be moved.

"Which one do you want, right or left?" asked Onewa.

"It makes no difference," said Nuju. "You choose."

One of the Kralhi stopped, as if listening to

The next instant, a jet of flame ...ped from its back, traveling rapidly down the length of its body. Before anyone could be quite sure what was happening, the two smoking halves of the machine collapsed.

Vakama returned to visibility then, lying on his back on the stone floor by Matau's feet. Using the Mask of Concealment to hide his movements, he had slid underneath the Kralhi and put his power of fire to good use.

Matau glanced down and grinned. "Then it's official, Toa-brother," he said. "You do more lying down than Onewa does all day."

A second Kralhi emerged from the shadows to join the lone surviving machine. But the Toa had no spare moments to worry about them. Mavrah's army of sea creatures had reached the shore, far faster than anyone had expected. The tentacles of a jellyfish-like creature erupted from the water, wrapped around Nokama's legs, and began pulling her into the lake.

Nuju reacted instantly, racing to use his ice powers against the creature. Before he could raise his crystal spikes, he was slammed by the powerful tail of a Rahi and flung across the cave.

Then it was Onewa's turn, reaching out with his Mask of Mind Control to seize control of the creature. Surprisingly, the Rahi fought back. It was left to Whenua to fend off attacks aimed at the Toa of Stone while Onewa remained locked in a mental struggle with the beast. Eventually, the Toa's will won out, as the Rahi released Nokama and dove beneath the water.

Onewa helped her to her feet. "Are you all right?"

Nokama nodded. "Yes, thanks to you. Another moment and I would have had to use my blades, and I don't like hurting living creatures."

"Well, you don't want to know what that thing thinks about," the Toa of Stone said, with a shudder. "You would never go fishing again."

Nokama looked around at the chaos breaking loose around her. Vakama and Matau were fighting off both the Kralhi and a half dozen flying Rahi rays. Nuju was still waiting for the world to stop spinning. Whenua had his hands full with an undersea insectoid that was larger than him and twice as strong. And all the while, there was Mavrah urging the creatures on.

"Help Whenua, and get Nuju back on his feet. We need him," Onewa said. "I am going to end this once and for all."

Despite himself, Mavrah was filled with joy. His friends had come when he called, just like he knew they would. Oh, they hadn't beaten these Toa yet, but they would. Then everything would be right again.

"Matoran!"

Mavrah turned. The one called Onewa was approaching, and he looked angry. The Matoran looked around, but there was nowhere to run. Instead, he stood his ground, refusing to show fear to some rock basher from Po-Metru.

"This ends now," said the Toa. "Call off your oversized aquarium before I show you what stone power can really do."

The Matoran laughed. "And if you trap me or knock me unconscious, what happens to your friends? Who will keep my Rahi from running wild? No, Onewa, accept it: you cannot harm me."

Onewa whirled at a familiar sound, one he had hoped never to hear again. "Maybe I can't, Mavrah," he said. "But they can."

The Matoran looked up. Fifteen Vahki Vorzakh had appeared above the lake, Staffs of Erasure at the ready, pausing while they decided whether to attack the Rahi or the Toa first. It was the sort of choice a Vahki loved.

A sea creature rammed the base of the rocky ledge on which Onewa and Mavrah stood. The Matoran fell backward into the cave, while Onewa pitched forward and hit the water. It was only after he was under the waves that he remembered that stone does not float . . . it sinks.

Onewa lay on the bottom of the lake. He had already taken a mouthful of water and his sluggish limbs would not allow him to rise. In his mind, he was back in Po-Metru at his carving table putting the finishing touches on a Kanohi mask. It was slow going. Every time he tapped his chisel into the mask, water gushed forth from it.

Still, there was no rush. Unlike with most projects, Onewa felt no sense of urgency to complete the work on this mask. Rather, he was strangely calm. Something deep inside of him was screaming that he needed to stop working and get out of there, but the voice was so faint he ignored it.

After all, what could be so terribly wrong?

Mavrah sat up, shaking off the effects of hitting

the hard stone floor. He opened his eyes, looked around, and wondered if he had lost his mind.

The sights and sounds of battle surrounded him. Vorzakh were challenging some of the monstrous Rahi. They had succeeded in using their stun staffs on the creatures in an effort to render them mindless. But erasing the minds of creatures that virtually had none to begin with accomplished little. The Rahi simply kept coming, knocking the startled Vorzakh out of the air and then dragging them underwater.

In the cave, four Toa Metru had formed a square, keeping their backs to each other. Elemental energies flashed as they defended themselves against Kralhi, Rahi, and Vahki. So far, no attack had gotten through to them, but they were so hard-pressed that they could not go on the offensive.

Mavrah's eyes widened as a Vorzakh veered sharply to the left and smashed into the stone wall. Sparking wildly, it slid into the water and vanished from sight. Nearby, Vakama and Nuju worked together against a Kralhi. While Nuju iced over half the machine, Vakama made the

other half glow white-hot. Whatever mechanisms the Kralhi used to compensate for ex-
tremes in temperature were rapidly fused or
frozen. The machine collapsed in on itself.

It was all too much. The roar of the Rahi,
the crackle of Vahki staffs, the howl of Matau's
winds combined to form an overwhelming wall
of sound. The Matoran winced as he saw a Vahki
slam into a Rahi, stunning it senseless and sending
the huge creature plunging into the water. He
turned away, only to see the four Toa being
driven back by a half dozen Vorzakh.

Four? he wondered. *I know Onewa disappeared in the water . . . but where is Whenua?*

The Toa of Earth was wondering the same thing.
He had spotted Onewa falling into the water.
When his comrade did not immediately resur-
face, Whenua dove in after him. Now he was
struggling to make his way through the turbulent
water and relying on his Mask of Night Vision to
light the way.

Residents of Onu-Metru and Po-Metru did

not normally form close friendships. Onu-Matoran were focused on the past, while Po-Matoran worried only about what work was due to be completed that day and how quickly they could get an akilini game going. But there was a connection between the two metru, whether their populations wanted to admit it or not. Both were bound to the ground, one mining the solid protodermis and the other turning it into the building blocks of the city.

Earth and stone were brothers, and Whenua knew it. So he never thought twice about risking his own life to save Onewa.

The beam from his Kanohi mask played across a strange shape on the bottom. It was Onewa, lying still, his heartlight dim and barely flickering. A school of Takea sharks was circling above the Toa of Stone, trying to determine if their prey was as defenseless as he seemed.

Whenua revved his earthshock drills and shot forward. The sharks scattered before him, confused by the vibrations in the water caused by his Toa tools. He knew he had only a few moments before they zeroed in again. A large ray tried to cut him off, but Whenua brushed it aside with a strength born of desperation.

He grabbed Onewa and pushed himself off the bottom, fighting to make the surface. The sharks turned and followed. Whenua could see the ledge so far above. With the precision of the archivist he used to be, he calculated that he was never going to make it in time.

The Toa of Earth kicked hard. If he was going to fail, he was going to fail giving it his best. In the back of his mind, he waited to feel the jaws of the sharks closing on his legs.

There was a stirring in the water. Whenua glanced to his left to see a huge Tarakava approaching, its powerful forearms already striking out. The creature was obviously heading for the two Toa, but the sharks were not willing to give up their hunt. They turned as one and began snapping at the large Rahi.

Hope flared anew in Whenua. He forced himself to swim the last few strokes and grabbed the ledge. With the last of his strength, he heaved

Onewa out of the water and on to solid ground. He was about to follow when a blow from the Tarakava struck him from behind. By sheer will, Whenua held on, dragging himself painfully back into the cave before collapsing.

Onewa coughed, spitting out water. He felt like he had been run over by a Kikanalo herd. Weak as he was, though, he found the energy to crawl to Whenua's side. The Toa of Earth was hurting, but still alive. Onewa glanced up to see Mavrah watching them.

"This is your friend," the Toa of Stone said, exhausted. "He might have been killed. Doesn't that mean anything to you?"

The Tarakava broke the surface, a shark clinging to one of its arms. Despite its advantages in size and strength, it was obvious the large Rahi would not survive.

"Or are you no better than them?" Onewa said, gesturing toward the lake.

"Don't," Mavrah answered. "They are my friends, my companions . . ."

Two flying fish closed in on a Vorzakh. It

moved out of the way at the last instant and the two Rahi began tearing at each other. "I see," said Onewa, contempt in his voice. "I see how you treat your friends. You put them in danger, you let them be hurt . . . I think I'd rather have you for an enemy."

A Vahki spiraled earthward, taking two Rahi with it. Vakama's flames drove a serpentine creature back under the water.

"Look around you," Onewa continued. "The Rahi you're supposed to be protecting are being wounded, even killed. None of this had to happen. You can stop it."

A Rahi with a head shaped like an axe blade smashed its way up through the cave floor, bowling over the four Toa. A giant crab, dazed by a Vahki stun blast, slipped off its ledge and fell into the water. A school of sharks made short work of it.

"But why bother?" said Onewa. "I mean, it was never about them anyway, right? It was about you. Dume was going to take your pet project away from you. No more secret passages, no more experiments, just back to the drudgery of working in the Archives. So you stole them and you slipped away, figuring — what? That you would find a way to make them tame, gentle little Ruki fish and return to Metru Nui as a hero of science?"

The axe-headed beast tossed Matau aside like he was made of seaweed. The Rahi underwater were locked in combat with each other, churning up the lake and sending huge waves crashing into the cave.

"You don't understand," Mavrah said weakly.

"I understand that my friends — beings who have risked their lives to save Matoran like you — are in danger," Onewa snapped. "I understand that your 'friends' have caught the scent of battle and are destroying each other. And I understand that this cave is going to be the last place any of us ever see in this lifetime."

Above their heads, the remaining Vahki were massing for another charge. The axe-headed marine creature had crushed the last Kralhi into a jumbled mess of machine parts.

Mavrah shook his head. "No, no. This isn't

what I wanted. This isn't how it's supposed to be." He ran for the ledge, yelling, "Stop it! Stop!"

Whenua, still shaken, tried to grab him and missed. "Mavrah, don't!"

But the Matoran was already at the edge of the water, waving his arms in vain. "Stop fighting! Please stop it!" Even if any of the combatants had been in the mood to listen, his words were drowned out by the sounds of battle and the roar of the waves.

Whenua got to his feet and staggered toward the Matoran. He had made it only two steps when the largest wave yet smashed into the ledge where Mavrah stood. One moment, the Onu-Matoran was there; the next, he was swept out into the violent waters.

The Toa of Earth charged forward, only to be grabbed by Onewa. "Whenua, no, it's too late," Onewa said. "The Rahi are out of control. You'll never find him in that. You'll be lost too."

"But he's my friend," Whenua said, even as

he realized that Onewa was right. Nothing could survive in the cauldron the lake had become.

"I know," Onewa replied. "And so am I."

Vakama looked up to see Onewa and Whenua running toward him. Nuju and Nokama had just finished driving the Rahi back underwater and sealing the hole in the cave floor with ice.

"Did you find the transport?" asked Onewa.

"Yes, it's not far."

"Then we need to go," said the Toa of Stone, "while we still can."

"What about the Vahki? Won't they ever-chase?" asked Matau.

Onewa shook his head. "Stop worrying, Ussal rider, and start running."

Vakama led the way through the tunnels and back to the transport. While the others got on board, Matau flew ahead to scout. He returned in a matter of moments with a rare piece of good news.

"All open-clear ahead," he reported. "This tributary bypasses the lake and the Rahi-beasts and feeds back into the river."

Whenua and Onewa pushed the transport off the rocky shelf and back into the water, then swiftly climbed on board. No one said anything about the missing Matoran sphere. They knew that if they did not get moving, the other five spheres would be lost as well, along with all hope for the sleeping Matoran back in Metru Nui.

Matau took the controls and they moved quickly down the tributary, each alone with their own thoughts. The sounds of battle faded, then grew louder again as they drew near the river. Then the transport shot through rapids and landed in another, wider tunnel. Behind them they could see the Rahi still battling Vahki and each other.

One airborne Vorzakh spotted the transport. Immediately, all thoughts of the fight were forgotten. Something was fleeing. Vahki were designed to chase anything that fled. It signaled to its companions and a half dozen Vahki took off after the Toa, rapidly gaining ground.

Vakama glanced over his shoulder and saw the mechanized guardians of Metru Nui closing in. "I'll slow them down," he said to Onewa. "You stop them."

"Do you know what you're asking?" answered the Toa of Stone. "We'll never be able to come this way again."

"Then we find another route!" Vakama said, loosing a barrage of fireballs on the oncoming Vahki. "We're going to find a new world, Onewa, and I don't want Vahki to be a part of it."

The Toa of Fire's elemental powers had not stopped the Vahki, but having to dodge his flames had delayed them and broken their formation. Onewa summoned all his energies and focused them on the roof of the tunnel. The rock was his to command, and by his will, a tunnel that had existed for ages began to collapse. The Vahki dodged the first stones, but the destruction continued, until finally the roof caved in all along the passage.

The Vahki disappeared beneath an avalanche of rock.

Matau brought the transport to a stop. All

six Toa Metru looked at the wall of stone that now blocked the tunnel. "I feel like that barrier is a sign," said Nokama quietly. "Almost as if the Great Spirit is telling us we will never return to Metru Nui."

"We'll go back," Vakama assured her. "We must. We still have a destiny to fulfill."

"Before we can go back, we have to go forward," said Whenua. "That was what Mavrah couldn't see. He became so fixed on what he might be losing, he forgot to look ahead to all the future might have held for him."

Nuju nodded. "Like so many Onu-Matoran . . . and too many Ko-Matoran . . . he tried to hide away from the world."

A Vahki staff floated to the surface of the water. Vakama fished it out and snapped it in two over his knee.

"But the world always finds you," the Toa of Fire said, discarding the pieces over the side of the *Lhikan*.

The transport idled in the water. The last few tight turns had damaged some of the legs and Whenua and Onewa were doing repairs. Nokama sat on the deck, her legs hanging over the side. She had cleaned Matau's "Makuta fish" and was using a sharpened rock to whittle at the bones.

"What are you making?" Vakama asked, sitting down beside her.

"A trident, like the Ga-Matoran fishcatchers use," she replied. "It will be a reminder of all we saw and experienced on this journey."

"I hope we are near the end. The water level in the tunnel is rising. It will be completely flooded soon."

Nokama paused to examine her work. "Do you think there will be other Toa where we are going, Vakama?"

The Toa of Fire shrugged. "I don't know. If

not, perhaps someday there will be. I'm sure our new home will have its share of dangers and the Matoran will need defenders."

"And we will be wise old Turaga," Nokama said, smiling. "Good for telling stories, judging akilini matches, and watching Matau try to fly a Gukko bird without falling off. Can't you just see it?"

She slipped off the transport and into the water. "I think perhaps we should leave this place a remembrance of us, for we won't pass this way again." Using the sharp edge of her hydro blade, she began to carve patterns in the rock wall.

When she was done, she turned to Vakama. "Not as good as what Onewa would do, but . . . what do you think?"

The Toa of Fire looked at the newly carved image of the six Toa Metru and smiled. "You should have been a Po-Matoran," he said. "It's a shame no one else will ever see this."

"It's amazing! Amazing!"

The two Toa turned to see Matau flying in excited circles above the ship.

"I found the new world-home! It's . . . it's . . . you have to come see!" the Toa of Air shouted.

"Can the transport get us there?" Vakama asked Onewa.

"If I say yes, will he stop yelling?"

"Probably."

"Then yes," said the Toa of Stone.

Long before they emerged from the tunnel, they were shielding their eyes from the light. Whenua, in particular, had to squint. "Mata Nui, if this place is so bright, how will we see anything?" he said.

Then suddenly they were out on the open sea again, with a whole new universe around them. Light, blazing like the fires of the Great Furnace, spilled down from a bright, yellow orb in the sky. The waters stretched out to the horizon, with no great stone barrier to enclose them. Above their heads, seabirds wheeled and screeched what might have been a welcome or a warning.

"By the Great Spirit . . . it's incredible," whispered Nokama. "Such beauty."

She reached down and caught some water in her cupped hand. Cautiously, she brought it to her mouth and took a taste. She immediately spat it back out. "This is *not* water," she said. "Not like what we knew on Metru Nui."

"You had best get used to surprises, Nokama," said Nuju. "I think this world is filled with them."

Matau turned the transport and for the first time, they saw the vast island that would be their new home. It was many times the size of Metru Nui, with mountains far higher than those of Po-Metru and great expanses covered with vegetation. At first, Vakama looked at all the plant life and wondered if perhaps this place was the domain of the Morbuzakh. Then he saw that the growing things here were lush and green, not withered and blackened like the vines that had menaced his city.

Nothing stirred on the beach. Beyond the birds overhead, there seemed to be no animal life on the island. The white sands looked as if no one had ever walked upon them before. All six Toa gazed upon the island with a mixture of awe, hope, and uncertainty.

"Where is the power plant?" asked Whenua. "Where are the chutes? The moto-hub? Even an assemblers' village would look good now."

"This is a wild place," said Vakama. "We are going to have build our own lives here, for ourselves and the Matoran, without the comforts of Metru Nui."

"Right," said Onewa, his voice heavy with sarcasm. "And then Matau will go live in a tree."

"The carver does have a point," said Nuju. "It is a wondrous place, but how can we expect the Matoran to live here? Can we build a civilization in this wilderness?"

"We'll find a way," said Vakama, with more confidence than Nokama could ever recall hearing in his voice. "That is why the Great Spirit Mata Nui guided us here and kept us safe on our journey. This will be our home and our haven."

"Then why do I feel like we have left a paradise behind, in favor of a very, very strange place?" asked Whenua. Then his attention was drawn to the seabirds, which looked like nothing he had ever seen before. "What do you think those are? We never had anything like that in the Archives. How do they glide on the air like that?"

"Well, Whenua is ready for our new land, I see," said Nokama. "I think the time has come, brothers."

Matau piloted the transport to shore. Nokama could not stop looking all around her, thinking what a wonderful spot this would make for a Ga-Matoran village. *Someday*, she thought, hopefully. *Someday I will bring them all here.*

Then, one by one, the Toa Metru stepped out onto the sands of the island that would be their home for many, many years to come.

EPILOGUE

"And so we found the island of Mata Nui, though it was not so called then," Turaga Nokama finished. "The Great Spirit had watched over us and helped us to find a place where the Matoran could live in peace once more."

"Then the carving I found in the underwater tunnel during my search for the Kanohi Nuva masks . . . the one of the six mysterious Toa —?" Gali Nuva began.

"That was the carving I made, long ago," said Nokama. "I led you there because I wanted you to find it, Gali. I wanted you to see you are not alone. You are part of a great tradition. There were heroes before you came, Toa of Water, and others will rise after your destiny is fulfilled."

Tahu Nuva spoke then, clearly uncomfortable about what he had to say. "I thank you for sharing your tale, Turaga. But my questions are still unanswered. You arrived on Mata Nui with only five Matoran, leaving so many behind in the depths of the city. How, then, did so many come to live here? Did they awaken and escape the city?"

Turaga Nuju clicked and whistled angrily at the Toa of Fire. Matoro looked at Turaga Nokama. "Do I have to translate that?" he asked. "I mean . . . he's a Toa, and when he gets angry, things burn."

"I am guessing Toa Tahu understands the spirit, if not the meaning, of Nuju's comments," Nokama replied. "I suppose all this is our own fault — first, for keeping secrets from you, and then for believing we could share some of our past while keeping other doors shut to you."

She turned to Nuju. "We should have remembered, my friend, that Toa cannot stand a closed door."

"Then there is more to the tale," said Tahu Nuva. "Why won't you reveal it?"

"Because it is not her tale to tell."

All present turned to see Turaga Vakama approaching. His expression was grim. Feeling the power and the wisdom that radiated from him, it was hard to believe he had ever been an uncertain Matoran forced into a hero's role.

"Tell me, Toa of Fire, of what are you most afraid?" the Turaga asked.

Tahu Nuva thought back on all the enemies he had faced: Makuta, the Bohrok, the Bahrag, the Bohrok-Kal, the Rahi, the Rahkshi. He remembered all the battles, lost and won, all the mysteries solved, all the dangers he had faced and overcome. But no easy answer to Vakama's question came to mind.

"If you fear nothing at all," said the Turaga, "then you are a fool and you will not understand my tale. It would be a waste of time to tell it."

In times past, Tahu would have reacted to such words with rage. But he had learned much about himself during the battle with Makuta and the Rahkshi. When he spoke, it was firmly and quietly. "Ignorance, Turaga."

"Explain."

"I worry . . . I am afraid . . . that one day I might lead my friends into danger — even cost them their lives — because I did not know all that I should have known."

Vakama smiled. "Then you are not a fool, Tahu. You are a leader, for that is what every leader dreads. I hope it is a nightmare you will never see come true."

At Vakama's words, Nokama and Nuju had turned away. There had been something in the tone of them that clutched at Gali's heart. For a moment, she wished that she could block all sound and not have to listen to the stories to come.

"You have heard tales of betrayal and hope," said Vakama. "Of power lost and power gained. From my lips, you have learned of the paradise that was the city of Metru Nui. Through my stories, you have faced Makuta once more, when his darkness was newly born."

The Turaga shook his head sadly. "But you know nothing of what that city became . . . nothing of true shadow . . . and nothing of the terrible choices a hero must make. Choices that must haunt his every waking hour for centuries."

Vakama looked up. In his eyes, Tahu could see some of the fire that had once been there when he was a Toa Metru, long ago.

"So this is what I will do for you, Tahu Nuva," the Turaga said. "I will tell you another tale, you and all of your fellow heroes of Mata Nui. I will spare no detail. And when I am done, you will have a choice. If you wish me to be silent, I will say no more and you can be content with what you know."

Vakama's tone grew as dark as Makuta's lair. "Or bid me speak on, Toa of Fire, and I will reveal to you the shapes in the shadows, and the true meaning of fear."

The Turaga turned and walked away, leaving Tahu, Gali and Kopaka to ponder the meaning of his words.